This Orchard book

belongs to

....

TEN LITTLE PRINCESSES

MIKE BROWNLOW SIMON RICKERTY

ORCHARD

Ten little princesses, going to the ball,

Trotting on their ponies, past the castle wall.

Are they looking forward to their very special day?

Ten little princesses all shout,

"Yay!"

Ten little princesses, looking quite divine.

"Ouch!"

– a princess pricks her thumb.

10

Now there are . . .

. . . **nine.**

Nine little princesses,

running rather late.

9

"Crunch!"

goes the poisoned apple.

Now there are . . .

...eight.

Eight little princesses pass a prince who's heaven.

"Hi,"

smiles the charming prince.

8

Now there are . . .

Seven little princesses
hide behind some sticks.

"**Huff!**"
blows a big bad wolf.

Now there are . . .

Now there are . . .

...**five.**

5

Five little princesses spot a hairy paw.

"You're a beauty," growls the Beast.

Now there are . . .

. . . four.

Four little princesses
climb a beanstalk tree.

4

"Fee-fie-foe!"

a giant says.

Now there are . . .

. . . three.

3

Three little princesses, really in a stew.

. . . two.

2

Two little princesses,
wondering where to run.

"Grrrr!"

snarls a sneaky troll.
Now there is . . .

One little princess, feeling sad and blue.

All her friends have disappeared.

Whatever can she do?

One little princess
makes a special call . . .
She rings her Fairy God Mum
on her mobile crystal ball.

Fairy God Mum waves her wand . . .

the others reappear!

The baddies run, the ball is saved.

It's time to whoop and cheer!

Ten little princesses all shout, "Yay!"

For my own little princesses, Dilly, Rachel, Sally and Catie
M.B.

For Erin and Isla
S.R.

ORCHARD BOOKS

First published in Great Britain in 2014 by Orchard Books
This edition published in 2015 by The Watts Publishing Group

12

Text © Mike Brownlow, 2014
Illustrations © Simon Rickerty, 2014

The moral rights of the author and illustrator have been asserted.

A CIP catalogue record for this book is available from the British Library.

ISBN 978 1 40833 012 8

Printed and bound in China

MIX
Paper from
responsible sources
FSC® C104740
FSC
www.fsc.org

Orchard Books
An imprint of
Hachette Children's Group
Part of The Watts Publishing Group Limited
Carmelite House
50 Victoria Embankment
London EC4Y 0DZ

An Hachette UK Company
www.hachette.co.uk

www.hachettechildrens.co.uk